THE SNOW ANGEL OF A DUKE

THE HOLIDAYS OF THE ARISTOCRACY
BOOK 5

LINDA RAE SANDE

The Gossip of an Earl

The Enigma of a Widow

The Secrets of a Viscount

The Widowers of the Aristocracy

The Dream of a Duchess

The Vision of a Viscountess

The Conundrum of a Clerk

The Charity of a Viscount

The Cousins of the Aristocracy

The Promise of a Gentleman

The Pride of a Gentleman

The Holidays of the Aristocracy

The Christmas of a Countess

The Knot of a Knight

The Holiday of a Marquess

The Winter Kiss of a Rogue

The Snow Angel of a Duke

The Heirs of the Aristocracy

The Angel of an Astronomer

The Puzzle of a Bastard

The Choice of a Cavalier

The Bargain of a Baroness

The Jewel of an Earl's Heir

The Vixen of a Viscount

The Honor of an Heir

The Rose of a Sultan's Son

The Ladies of the Aristocracy

The Lady of a Grump

The Lady of a Sultan

The Pursuit of a Duchess

The Wager of a Wallflower

The Lords of the Aristocracy

The Abduction of an Earl

Beyond the Aristocracy

The Pleasure of a Pirate

The Making of a Mistress

The Bride of a Baronet

The Caton of a Captain

Puss and Pots

The Betrothal of a Baron

Stella of Akrotiri

Origins

Deminon

Diana

The Lyon's Den (Dragonblade Publishing)

The Courage of a Lyon

The Lady of a Lyon

Note: Translations of select titles are available in German, Italian, Spanish and Portuguese.

CHAPTER 1
AN IMPRESSION IN
THE SNOW

December 1815, Dunfey Park, Westmorland

Andrew loved days like this. Snowy, cold, gray wintry days that required him to stay indoors. They were the best excuse to remain sequestered in his study seeing to ducal business or curled up in one of the chairs in the parlor reading a book whilst sipping tea or brandy.

Tea during the day and brandy at night.

Although there were times he could have easily imbibed all day long—drunkenness helped keep his phobia at bay—he had long ago learned he couldn't spend his waking moments in a fog.

He had responsibilities. A dukedom to run.

Even if he hadn't stepped foot on the property since he was six years old.

"Good morning, Your Grace. Would you like to dress now?"

The valet's voice had Andrew's attention turning from the master bedchamber's window. He hadn't been looking out of it, exactly. He rarely looked outside. "Oh, if I must," he replied on a sigh. "I hardly know why we bother."

Pruitt held out a pair of Nankeen breeches and a scarlet waistcoat. "Have you any appointments on this day?"

Andrew gave his servant a quelling glance. "Of course not. How would anyone even reach this place?" he asked, waving toward the window.

Besides the impending storm—gray clouds pregnant with snow were headed in their direction—the grounds appeared to be covered in a white blanket of powder that had been spread out the day before.

"I doubt a coach-and-four could get here," he added as removed his banyan and allowed Pruitt to dress him.

"I asked only because it seems someone—or something—has made its way onto the grounds, Your Grace."

Andrew stiffened as Pruitt wrapped a pleated cravat around his neck. "What are you saying?"

His valet angled his head towards the room's only window. "There's an impression in the snow. It appears..." He paused and furrowed a brow as he tied a knot into the ends of the silk. "You have to see it for yourself, Your Grace."

Glancing toward the window, Andrew tugged on the ends of his sleeves. From the amount of light that filtered into the bedchamber, he knew it was still sunny out. The snow only enhanced the brightness. "All right."

Although he generally stayed away from the windows—so much as stepping close to a pane of glass where he could make out the expanse beyond had his heart racing in his chest—he managed to make it to the drapes. Keeping his gaze directed down, he scanned the snow-covered grounds below and understood immediately what his valet meant by his comment.

"Is that... is that an angel?" he asked in awe. He took one more step, his attention so focussed on the snow below that he didn't notice he was fully exposed by the window.

"My thought exactly. As if one fell from the sky. Except..." The valet cleared his throat. "If you look off to the east, you can see some tracks in the snow."

The blinding white stuff had Andrew squinting as he turned his head and then his body in an attempt to follow the footsteps. They disappeared behind a snow-topped hedgerow that outlined the parterre garden on the east end of Dunfey Park. From his position three stories up, the garden's symmetrical design was evident despite the layer of white that covered it, the shapes further enhanced by what appeared to be glitter sprinkled over everything.

He couldn't remember having noticed the sparkles before, but then he usually didn't stare out windows.

"Well, an animal certainly didn't do it," he reasoned, finally stepping away from the cold glass. A bank of storm clouds suddenly hid the sun, and the snow lost its blinding white brilliance.

"Should I send a footman to determine who might have trespassed?" Pruitt asked, holding the topcoat open.

Andrew slipped his arms into the sleeves and shook his head. "No need. There's been no harm done."

"Very good, Your Grace. Your breakfast should be ready."

"I don't suppose any mail has been delivered? Or a copy of the *Times*?" he asked. He made his way out of the bedchamber and to the stairs, Pruitt following close behind.

"No, Your Grace. If it stays as cold as it's been, the snow won't melt. We may have to send Smithton into town to fetch the mail," he replied, referring to one of the footmen.

"We'll give it another day," Andrew said, deciding news from London could wait. As for instructions he had wished to send to his dukedom's foreman, he had another day in which to write them.

Not that he had plans to go anywhere.

Andrew, Duke of Suffolk, had never stepped foot out of Dunfey Park.

CHAPTER 2
ESCAPING AN ANGEL

eanwhile, to the east of Dunfey Park

Her labored breaths sending out clouds of white in front of her chilled face, Angelika raced toward Stonefield Manor. She was sure someone would be following her at any moment. There was no where to hide and no way to cover her tracks.

The snow was too deep. Even holding up her redingote and skirts, their hems were skimming the soft powder that blanketed the ground for as far as she could see.

She had to squint to do so, it was so bright. The cold air made breathing difficult, and she could practically see crystals forming in front of her face with every breath. Glittery sparkles that were there one second and gone the next.

Daring a glance back, she slowed her steps. She didn't hear any shouts. She didn't see anyone at all.

Someone at Dunfey Park had seen her, though. He had probably been watching her the entire time she was in front of the parterre garden, making a fool of herself as she created a snow angel.

With such pristine powder, forming a snow angel was easy. Angelika simply fell backward into the snow and waved her arms and legs. Harder to do was attempting to escape the angel without disturbing the surrounding snow. She had devised a way to do so, though. She left a pair of footprints at the bottom edge of the angel's skirts before taking as large a leap as possible away from the impression.

Grinning at the embossed shape she had created, she was about to take her leave when she realized she was being watched.

An older man, his face framed in a window, was staring at her as she stepped away from the snow angel.

Although she couldn't be sure of his expression— he didn't seem angry but mayhap amused—she decided he couldn't have been the master of the house. Not given the tales some in town told of the reclusive duke who lived at Dunfey Park.

The Duke of Suffolk was said to have never left his house because he was hideous. Because he had suffered some sort of awful accident that left him disfigured. That as a result, he was a beast.

The man in the window didn't appear to have anything wrong with him. *Probably the butler,* she reasoned as she continued on her way home.

Besides, even if the duke had some sort of disfigurement, how bad could it be? Having read enough gothic novels in her twenty years, she could imagine a horrid beast. She also knew from those novels that a horrific looking creature wasn't always horrible in his manners, so the duke's outward appearance probably wasn't necessarily an indication of how he behaved in polite company.

As to whether or not the Duke of Suffolk behaved as a gentleman, no one seemed to know from first-hand experience. There were those in town who claimed very few in Westmorland had even met the man, he was so secretive. None of Angelika's acquaintances admitted to having spoken so much as a single word with the duke, so how would they know?

She glanced back over her shoulder again, disappointment settling over her. She hadn't expected to actually see the duke on this day, but that didn't mean she wouldn't have welcomed a hint of what he looked like.

Passing the line of poplar trees that separated the

duke's Dunfey Park estate from that of her father's marquessate, Angelika was reminded of his recent letter —the last bit of mail the Royal Mail coach had delivered before the snow had deepened so much, coaches could no longer reach nearby Kirkby Kendal.

> *Dear Angel,*
>
> *I pray this letter finds you in good health and warm at Stonefield Manor.*
>
> *Your brother arrived on British shores a week ago bearing tanned skin and an extra trunk filled with treasures from his trip. It seems Greece and the Kingdom of the Two Sicilies agreed with him, for he is at least two inches taller than when he left and at least a stone heavier. You might not recognize him.*
>
> *As for when you'll see us, that is a matter of which I cannot be sure.*
>
> *Although I hoped Robert's arrival might bring with it some warm Mediterranean weather, it has not. The sunsets have become rather brilliant, though, when there are not clouds blocking the western vantage.*
>
> *Winter has descended with a vengeance here in the capital, and I have learned from colleagues it is the same in other parts of the country. My*

plan is still to make it back to Stonefield Manor for Christmas, but if the snows are too deep for our traveling coach, or if I learn the coaching inns are closed due to the foul weather, I may have to delay our departure from the capital.

Please do not despair if we are delayed. We shall celebrate Christmastide whenever Robert and I make it there. In the meantime, do continue seeing to the household as you always have. I promise to bring you even more books than you asked for when I left.

All my love,

Your father

The thought of more books had Angelika grinning as she made her way to the front door of Stonefield Manor. The butler, Bronson, had it opened before she had a chance to use the boar's head brass knocker. A good thing, too, for she could barely feel her fingers.

"You were out there far too long, my lady," Bronson scolded. He watched as she struggled to undo the buttons of her redingote.

"Perhaps," she replied. "But it was invigorating."

"I asked cook to see to it tea would be ready upon your return. Styles has finally come back from town—"

"Was there any mail?"

He shook his head. "No coaches have come into town from any direction in the past two days."

Disappointment settled over Angelika, but she tried hard not to let it show. "Well, then we shan't expect Father and Robert for a few more days, then," she said brightly, feigning nonchalance. "Do you suppose Styles and Thompkins can collect a yule log? Some greens?" Although it was still another week before Christmas Eve—the day they would normally bring in evergreens with which to make the wreaths and sprays that would decorate the front hall and the parlor—she worried the weather might prevent them from doing so.

"They have already seen to cutting a tree, my lady. And some greenery. They have the branches stored in a bucket of water in the stable."

"It's probably frozen by now," she remarked, allowing him to help with her redingote.

"Do you want them to bring the greens inside?" he asked, worry evident on his face.

"Oh, no," she answered quickly. "They'll be fine where they are until the twenty-fourth." If it wasn't considered bad luck to bring them in early, she would welcome the opportunity to work on wreaths and sprays, if for no other reason than it would help counteract the boredom she had experienced since a week after her father's departure.

Although she loved reading books, even reading would become a chore if there was nothing else to do. Besides, she had finished all the novels and was now having to read books on botany, animal husbandry, and modern farming techniques.

Her thoughts briefly went back to the Duke of Suffolk. If the man never stepped foot outside of Dunfey Park, then he must have a good number of projects to keep him occupied.

Could running a dukedom require his attention all of the time, though? What else might a recluse do all day besides read books and eat? Write letters and read newspapers?

Make love.

Angelika blinked.

From where had that thought come?

She knew, actually, but that didn't mean she wanted anyone else in the household to know she had discovered her father's books on the subject. That she had spent the day before pouring over pages of explicit descriptions and illustrations that had her wincing as much as they had her excited.

Sure her face was bright red, and not only because

of the cold, she made her way through the hall and up the marble stairs to the parlor. A fire crackled in the fireplace, and she rushed over to warm her hands.

Bronson soon joined her, setting the tea tray on the low table next to her favorite chair. "Will there be anything else, my lady?"

"No, Bronson. I shall wrap myself in a blanket and read until it's time for dinner," she replied. "And I shan't be dressing for dinner tonight," she added, deciding the practice made no sense when she would be the only one at the dinner table.

She briefly thought of her younger brother. He was no doubt upstairs with his nurse, either playing with his wooden toys or learning to read. "I think Richard should join me for dinner tonight." The young boy rarely had a chance to eat in the dining room, but he needed to learn his dining manners at some point.

"Very good, my lady."

She watched the servant depart, then reached under the upholstered chair cushion. She pulled out a French book on the topic of sexual congress.

She could read the French text, of course, but she planned to spend the time studying the color plates in the middle. The scandalous paintings would warm her up faster than standing in front of the fire.

Pulling the blanket around her shoulders, she

settled into the chair and opened the book to the center, where page after page displayed paintings depicting men and women in various positions. Although most couples were shown atop a bed, some were set in other rooms of a house, including a library, and one was even in a folly—in broad daylight.

The thought of being out-of-doors, mostly naked, shocked her more than the strange positions shown in any of the other paintings.

Most shocking of all, though, was imagining what it might be like to make love to a man so disfigured, he was considered a beast. Angelika was almost relieved when Bronson appeared to announce dinner was served.

Tucking the book back under the cushion, she made her way downstairs in a daze, well aware it was once again snowing.

Dressed in his best clothes, Richard stood at the bottom of the stairs, his huge grin making it appear as if a pugilist had knocked out his front teeth.

"Good evening, Sister," he said before she was even halfway down the flight of stairs.

"Good evening to you, Richard. You look terribly happy." She felt a twinge of guilt at not have changed for dinner, but the boy didn't seem to notice.

"That's because I am," he said, holding out his

elbow as high as he could when she joined him. "Nurse says Christmas is in a week."

Angelika placed her arm on his elbow and allowed him to lead her into the dining room, relieved to see that the place settings were set across the short side of the long table. Had they been placed at the ends, it would have made conversation difficult for the two youngest children of Mark, Marquess of Stonely.

Richard pulled out a chair for her before moving to his own. One of the footmen, Thompkins, lifted the boy onto his chair, one that had two large books resting on the seat, and then pushed it closer to the table.

"You can serve the wine and the first course now," Angelika said, her attention on the footman.

"Yes, my lady."

"Do I have to drink wine?" Richard asked, a grimace wrinkling his nose.

"No. I'm sure cook has made something with milk for you," she replied. Despite the cold, the cow continued to provide milk for the household.

Thompkins served the soup and poured wine for her. He set a silver mug of warm caudle before Richard, and Angelika inhaled softly.

"Cook assures me she didn't add very much in the way of spirits to his drink," the footman said when he noticed her reaction.

"Very good, Thompkins," she said, not about to ask if she might have some, too. Given the time of year and her brother's lean frame, she knew cook was doing her best to fatten up the boy.

"I received a letter from Father." She watched as her brother correctly used the larger spoon to lift soup from his bowl. He managed to get it to his mouth without spilling it down his front. "Robert has returned to London. They're going to do everything they can to make it here in time for Christmas."

Richard's eyes rounded. "Robert?" he repeated.

"Our older brother."

He seemed to think on her response a moment before he asked, "Is he the one who used to come here for dinner sometimes?"

Angelika chuckled softly. "Yes. He actually lived here..." She stopped when she realized Robert had been away for most of Richard's life, for school at Eton, then university, and finally his Grand Tour. "We'll have to reintroduce you two when he comes home," she added.

"I remember him when he was last here for a district ball."

"You do?" she asked in surprise. "That would have been two years ago." Their father hosted the annual event at Stonefield Manor, a means by which to gather the members of the nearby landed gentry for an evening of dancing and a midnight supper. Ever since her mother had died, Angelika had been responsible for the arrangements and invitations. "Shouldn't you have been in bed at that time of the evening?"

Richard grinned. "I was supposed to be, but I was watching. From upstairs. Mrs. Cooper said she was going to be with her husband that night, so I didn't go to bed until after everyone left."

Scoffing, Angelika regarded her brother with a smirk. "Were you now? So... were you watching the dancing? Or...?"

He shrugged. "The dancing and the kissing."

Angelika blinked. "Kissing? Do you mean Mr. and Mrs. Cooper?" Although the two had been married for longer than she had been alive, Angelika couldn't imagine the two involved in anything as intimate as a kiss.

Furrowing his brows, Richard shook his head and made a sound of disgust. "No. Not them." He was about to say more, but the footman appeared with the next course.

Although she was curious as to who her brother had paid witness to kissing during the ball, she thought it best she didn't encourage him to share gossip. Her father had always said men were the worst gossips, and she was beginning to understand why.

They ate in companionable silence for a time, Richard determined to finish his soup before the footman could remove his bowl.

"Has Mrs. Cooper taken you outdoors today?" she asked when Thompkins appeared with their main course. Cook had dished up the plates in the kitchen, and Angelika was relieved to see steam rising from the vegetables. Tonight's dinner would be hot.

"Not today," he replied. "She said it was too cold."

"It is cold, but it makes the snow all soft and powdery."

"I saw you making a snow angel," he said. "I was looking out the window. Will you teach me how?"

Angelika scoffed. "I do every year," she reminded him, a brow arching in a tease.

"Did you make more than one today?

"Of course," she replied. "West of here. The snow was perfect."

"Did you go to Dunfey Park?"

Angelika froze in her chair, her fork halfway to her mouth. "Now why would you ask that?"

"I saw you through the window," Richard claimed. "I saw you walk past the line of popular trees."

"Poplar trees," she corrected. She sighed and added, "I suppose my walk did take me onto the Dunfey Park property."

"Nurse says the duke is a recluse." Although his attention was on his roast beef, Richard paused to regard her with a quizzical expression. "What is a recluse?"

Angelika considered how to respond. "Did nurse say anything else about the duke?"

Richard shrugged. "He doesn't go outside. She says it's because he's ugly, even though he's not old."

Wincing, she made a clucking sound with her tongue. "A recluse is someone who stays indoors and prefers his own company, and it's not nice to say someone is ugly."

"Nurse says people go to him, though, so does that still make him a recluse?"

Placing her fork on her plate, she leaned forward. "What people?"

He shrugged again. "A man. He comes in a coach. Always leaves 'afore nurse—"

"Before," she corrected him.

"Before nurse feeds me dinner."

"How often?"

"Two times every month. Usually on a Friday. In the morning."

Angelika blinked. "How do you know this?" she asked in alarm.

"I can see his coach from my window," he replied.

"He carries a leather case like Father does. Nurse says it's his man of business."

Remembering the nursery was on the top floor of the house, Angelika understood how it was her brother could see the duke's property. But someone actually *on* the property? "You can see that far?"

"With Father's looking glass I can."

"You've been *spying* on our neighbor?" she asked, her mouth open in shock. Why she hadn't thought to use the looking glass for the same purpose had her momentarily flummoxed.

He nodded. "When nurse thinks I'm taking a nap," he affirmed, finally stabbing a boiled potato with his fork after several failed attempts.

"Have you ever seen the duke?"

Richard shrugged. "Don't know. Never saw anyone who was ugly, though."

"Richard," she scolded.

"Have *you* seen him?" he asked. Although he was keeping up his end of the conversation, he seemed more interested in the food on his plate.

Angelika remembered the man who had been watching her from the window. "I don't think so," she murmured. "But I think I should like to make his acquaintance."

His eyes rounding in surprise, her brother said, "What if he is ugly?"

She shrugged. "I have done enough reading in my life to know that one shouldn't judge a book by its cover," she replied. "I do believe the same goes for people."

Richard didn't appear convinced as he chewed. After he swallowed, he took a sip from his caudle and said, "Well, tomorrow is Friday, so you'll have to wait until the afternoon."

Blinking, Angelika was about to claim she had no intention of going to meet the duke without their father —surely the marquess and the duke knew each other— and then thought better of it. Perhaps she could meet him under different circumstances.

Unplanned planned circumstances.

CHAPTER 3
CAUGHT... IN MORE WAYS THAN ONE

The following day, Friday, December 15, 1815

Dressed in her warmest woolen dress, her feet encased in two pairs of stockings and her highest boots, Angelika set out for an afternoon walk. With any luck, she might attract the duke's attention, or come upon him if he was on a stroll in his gardens.

Who was she kidding? The snow was at least six inches deep. Someone would have to be desperate for a walk to do what she was doing.

Her father would say it was good for the constitution. Had he been at Stonefield Manor, he might very well have joined her on the trek west.

Although it wasn't nearly as cold as the day before,

it had snowed overnight. Her tracks from the day before were barely visible.

Until she passed the line of poplar trees that separated the two estates, she was forced to keep her steps slow. The snow was a bit deeper on the slightly inclined hill closer to Stonefield Manor, and her boot prints from the day before were almost completely filled in with new white powder.

She had almost stepped into the boxwood hedge of the parterre garden when she looked up to discover the east side of the Portland stone manor house of Dunfey Park looming above her. Redirecting her steps to go around the formal garden, she headed north toward the back of the property.

Off in the distance, she could make out a folly on the shore of a frozen pond. A circle of marble columns jutted from the snow to a domed roof patterned after a Greek tholos. Topped with snow, it looked much a like the frozen ices served at Gunter's Tea Shop in Berkeley Square.

The folly reminded her of the color plate she had seen in the French book, and an odd sensation of pleasure rolled through her middle. Perhaps distance, coupled with the columns, would provide enough privacy for a clandestine encounter. Not now, though. It was entirely too cold to be doing any sort of love-making out of doors. Not that she had anyone with which to do anything so scandalous.

About to turn around and make her way back home, her gaze swept over the ground around her. She inhaled softly. Unspoiled snow surrounded her. She took a large step forward, turned around, and fell backwards with a yelp of delight. The powdery snow sprayed out around her as she waved her arms. For a moment, she remained flat on her back, staring up at a sky that had been blue but was now quickly disappearing behind a bank of clouds.

She sat up, careful not to disturb the impression she had made as she struggled to stand. As she used her gloved hands to wipe away the snow from her redingote, she realized she was being watched.

Framed by the back door of the manor house, a man stood wearing a black cape coat, his hands shoved in his pockets. A fashionable top hat added another eight inches to his average height, which she decided made him about the same size as her father.

I've been discovered.

The thought brought with it two options. She could run. Her progress would be impeded by the snow that blanketed the land between here and Stonefield Manor.

The other option was to simply own up to what she had done. Curtsy. Apologize. Say she would never do it again. Walk slowly back to Stonefield Manor and hope the owner of the property didn't pay a call on her father with his complaint about her having trespassed.

"Please, don't run away."

The man's words had Angelika blinking.

Perhaps there was a third option.

She curtsied and gazed at him for a moment. When he didn't say anything else, she said, "Very well."

She knew right away this was probably not the same man who had spotted her from an upper story window the day before, for he had been much older than this handsome man. Or perhaps it was the same man, and seeing him without a pane of glass separating them made him appear younger. Five-and-thirty, mayhap. No. Thirty.

What did she know about men's ages, though? She hadn't met enough of them in her life to gauge their ages.

"From where have you come?" he asked, his gaze darting about as if he'd never been in the back gardens before. Given this year's deep snow, perhaps he hadn't seen it like this.

"Stonefield Manor, sir," she replied. "Next door."

He furrowed a brow.

"The Marquess of Stonely," Angelika offered. The man must be new to Westmorland.

"Oh. Of course. I'd quite forgotten about his country estate," he replied, his back pressed against the door as if he required it to stand.

"I hope you don't mind. What I've been doing. You have such pristine snow here, you see."

He shook his head. "I don't mind. I did wonder, though, what exactly it is that you're doing?"

Angelika blinked. "Making snow angels, sir."

"Snow angels," he repeated, not making it a question.

She nodded. "Would you like to join me?"

He once again glanced around and appeared to have trouble breathing. "Uh… yes," he finally said. "Might I ask what I should call you?"

Had they been in London, she knew never to engage in a conversation with a strange man unless she had a chaperone with her. Out here, she didn't have the protection of her father or older brother. Nor was there anyone to perform an introduction. "Angelika," she replied with a nod. "Or just Angel, if you'd like." She moved closer, expecting he might take her hand to his lips. She hoped he might.

"Angel," he repeated softly. "I am Andrew." He

seemed about to say more but paused. "It's very good to meet you."

"And you, sir," she said, curtsying again. When he didn't step forward to take her hand, her eyes darted to the side. "I take it you haven't made a snow angel before?" she asked.

He shook his head. "I haven't had the pleasure."

"Well, it's very easy. You simply fall back into the snow and wave your arms and legs," she explained. She did a quick demonstration for him, which had his eyes rounding in alarm as she spread out her arms and fell backwards. "The hardest part is getting back onto your feet without disturbing the snow."

He finally stepped away from the door and offered a gloved hand. From the condition of the black leather, it appeared as if it had never been worn before. She placed her kid leather-gloved hand in his and allowed him to help her to stand.

"Thank you, Andrew." She took an exaggerated step to the side and turned to examine her work. "What do you think?" She glanced to her left and realized he was no longer next to her but had returned to the door, his eyes closed and his head leaning back so his top hat touched the wood.

"Are you all right?" she asked, hurrying to stand before him.

"I will be," he replied. "In a moment."

Angelika furrowed a strawberry blonde brow. "Perhaps a walk will help?"

His eyes popped open. "I really wish that were the case," he whispered. In a louder voice, he added, "Would you take my arm? Lead the way?" He bent one arm, but both hands were shoved into his greatcoat pockets.

That's when she noticed the condition of his coat—the black wool looked as if it had never been worn before. All the buttons were in place, and none hung as if the threads were loose.

She considered the odd request and then wrapped her hand around his elbow. "Like this?"

He nodded. "Where are we going?"

"Where would you like to go?"

Closing his eyes, he said, "To the edge of the property."

Angelika grinned. "Well, that's not far," she claimed, pointing to the line of poplar trees. The path she had taken to his back garden was clearly marked by her footsteps in the snow.

"Lead the way," he said, squaring his shoulders.

Thinking perhaps he had recently recovered from an injury, Angelika took an experimental step forward, then another. She noted how he kept pace, his attention on his booted feet. If she hadn't been leading the way, he would have walked directly into one of the supports of an arbor arch.

"Have you lived here long?" she asked in an effort to keep up her end of the conversation.

"Since I was six years old," he replied.

She had to stutter step in the snow when he almost stopped. "Except for a few months in London every few years, I have lived at Stonefield my entire life. How is it we haven't met before?"

His boots shuffled in the snow as if he feared slipping and falling, his steps half the length of hers. "I don't get out much."

Pausing to look around, Angelika grinned and said, "This would be a perfect location for a snow angel. Would you like to try?"

A sliver of sun suddenly brightened the snow. Andrew glanced up and his eyes closed as the light illuminated his features. A grin split his face.

Angelika inhaled softly, struck by how happy he seemed. "Oh, it's so good to see the sun again…" She stopped speaking when his grin disappeared and his eyes went white. A second later, he fell backwards, his body ramrod straight. He sunk into the snow a few inches but didn't wave his arms or legs.

From the way her late Aunt Charity frequently

fainted, Angelika knew immediately he had done the same.

"Andrew!" she cried out.

*O*f course it was too good to be true. That this beautiful young woman could keep his attention on anything other than the fact that he was outside —out-of-doors—for more than five minutes. If only he could keep his eyes downcast. To imagine the snow was merely white carpeting. That the gray clouds above were simply a painted ceiling in a large ballroom.

As soon as the sun had appeared in a rather small break in the clouds, he had glanced up. His imaginary safety net dissipated as the sun's rays hit his face and he saw the awful clouds surrounding the ball of light.

Although it had felt good to feel the sun like that, it was also a reminder that he was outside. The protection of indoors was gone. Memories from when he was six invaded his mind. Terrified him, much as they had done back then.

Instead of crying out in fear or burying his head into Angelika's shoulder to block out the sensation, he succumbed to it, his eyes rolling up. The sense of vertigo overwhelmed him, and he fell back, his arms spread out as if they might be able to stop his downward descent.

Expecting a hard landing, he was pleasantly surprised when it felt as if he had fallen into a large pillow. Despite a faraway voice calling his name, he allowed the darkness of sleep to take him.

CHAPTER 4
A REASON IS SHARED

*M*eanwhile…

"Sir? Andrew?" Angelika shook the prone man's shoulders before moving a hand to the side of his face. "Andrew! Wake up," she said in a louder voice. About to lift his head from the snow, she heard someone call out.

An older man approached, his hurried steps slowed by the snow. "What's happened?" He landed on his knees on the other side of Andrew.

"I think he fainted," she replied, her eyes rounding with worry. "Do you know him?"

"I am his valet, miss. Pruitt is my name."

"I am Lady Angelika Westbrook. My father is Lord Stonely."

"My lady," he responded, nodding once. "I fear I cannot lift him by myself."

"I can get help. My house is just there," she said, pointing down the slight incline to where the three-story Lazonby sandstone manor house jutted from the ground, its green slate roof covered in snow. "And we have footmen," she added. "Stay with him. I'll be right back."

She hurried off, following her own footprints in the snow as she held up her skirts and dashed through the powder. Bursting through the front door, she called out, "I need help!"

Bronson appeared from the butler's pantry, a look of alarm on his face. "My lady?"

"I need the two footmen. Styles, especially. A man has passed out near the poplars." She struggled to catch her breath. "Prepare a bedchamber for him. A good one," she added. If the man had a valet, then he probably wasn't simply landed gentry or a visitor to Dunfey Park as she had suspected.

Was he, in fact, the master of Dunfey Park?

"I'll see to it right away," the butler assured her, pointing to a tall footman who had already appeared from the back of the house upon hearing her cry for help.

"Follow my footsteps in the snow, toward the tree line," Angelika instructed before hurrying up the steps and into the parlor. She gathered the blanket she had been wrapped in the day before and rushed out of the house.

The footman, Styles, was already on his way, his long legs giving him a distinct advantage over Angelika. He had Andrew up and leaning against him when she arrived to wrap the blanket around his back. Breathless, the second footman, Thompkins, joined them.

Between the two of them, they carried Andrew to the house, Pruitt and Angelika following close behind.

"Who is he?" she asked, her expression conveying worry.

Pruitt furrowed a graying brow. "He did not introduce himself?"

"He said his name was Andrew."

The valet didn't bother trying to hide his surprise at hearing her response. "His Grace, the Duke of Suffolk."

Angelika blinked. "I've been teaching a *duke* how to make snow angels?" she asked in disbelief. She glanced back to where Andrew had fallen into the snow. Despite the marks made by her knees and those of the valet's, the impression of the duke's body had left a near-perfect angel.

"I admit to wondering if that is what you two had been doing," Pruitt replied. "You must have been the one to decorate the grounds with an angel only yesterday."

Despite the cold, Angelika's face warmed. "It was me," she admitted. "The snow is pristine on the property there. The top isn't crusted over as it is in front of Stonefield." She inhaled softly. "What's wrong with him?"

The valet swallowed and took a deep breath. A cloud of white surrounded him when he exhaled. "His Grace does not do well out-of-doors."

Frowning, Angelika tried to understand. "He doesn't like the sun?"

"Oh, he likes it. He just cannot tolerate being outside. In the open."

"Because he doesn't like the out-of-doors? Or...?"

"He suffers from a condition, my lady. There is no hope for it, which is why I find it so surprising he left the house today."

Bronson had the front door open and escorted them to a first floor bedchamber, where a maid had pulled down the counterpane and bed linens and had started a fire in the fireplace.

Styles assisted Pruitt in removing the duke's greatcoat and topcoat. He lifted him onto the bed while Thompkins helped to straighten him. Carefully folding the top coat, Pruitt hung it over the back of a chair while Bronson draped the duke's wet greatcoat over his arm.

Covering the duke with the bed linens, Angelika moved to the head of the bed and gently lifted his head to place a pillow under it. The two footmen stepped aside, leaving the room when the butler shoo'd them out.

"Might I stay in here? I think it best I be here when His Grace awakens," Pruitt said.

"Of course. Please, do have a seat," Angelika said. She turned to Bronson. "Will you bring tea? Biscuits, too, and broth, if cook has any."

"Yes, my lady. I'll see to drying his coat." He gave a nod and left the bedchamber, closing the door behind him.

She leaned over the edge of the bed and placed the back of her hand against Andrew's forehead.

For a moment, she was overcome with emotion. She remembered when she discovered him watching her from the back door of Dunfey Park. How her momentary fear had been replaced with the certainty he meant her no harm. How he had looked up the moment when the clouds had parted and the sun's rays had hit the snow and made it look as if it was covered with glitter. How for the briefest of moments, an expression of awe had lit his features—or perhaps it was merely the sunlight—before the clouds once again hid the sun and his eyes seemed to roll up into the back of his head. That was before he collapsed backwards into the snow.

There was no evidence of a fever, and the duke's features had softened. He looked so peaceful. So handsome. Not the least bit disfigured. Surely not a beast.

The thought of seeing him like this every day had the oddest sensations coursing through her body. To wake up and have him be the first thing she saw would certainly be an excellent way to start the day.

"What you said earlier, about being surprised he would leave the house?" Angelika asked in a quiet voice. "Why do you suppose he did?"

Having moved to an upholstered chair near the fireplace, Pruitt stood next to it and finally allowed a shrug. "He is quite taken with you, my lady," he murmured. "I believe his curiosity helped him overcome his fear. At least for a time."

"Hmm." She pulled a chair to the side of the bed and settled onto it, resting her forearms on the edge of the mattress.

Once she was seated, Pruitt sat and buried his face in his hands.

"What's wrong, Mr. Pruitt?"

Embarrassed by having been caught in such a state, the valet quickly straightened in the chair. "I had hoped by this time in his life, the duke would have recovered from his malady," he replied. "Instead, he seems no better than when he was a child."

Furrowing her brows, Angelika considered his words. "Since he was six years old?" she guessed.

Pruitt's eyes rounded. "How did you know?"

Her attention went back to Andrew. "He mentioned something about living in that house since he was six."

Audibly sighing, the valet seemed reluctant to offer more information until Angelika arched a brow. "His father moved him there. After his mother died," Pruitt stated.

She swallowed, remembering very well the day her own mother had died giving birth to her younger brother. Her father hadn't been the same since, his manner that of an overprotective parent when it came to his children. Deciding London wasn't safe, he moved her and Richard to Stonefield Manor, where they had lived ever since, while Robert continued his schooling.

Mark Westbrook had to be cajoled and coerced by a fellow aristocrat to allow Robert to leave England for his Grand Tour. Until his recent return, their father worried himself sick about his eldest son's fate.

At some point in the next fortnight, Robert and the marquess would return to Westmorland for Christmas and the Twelve Days, Angelika's favorite time of the year.

"How did she die?" she asked, settling back in her chair.

Pruitt glanced at the duke, as if to ensure he was still passed out, before he said, "An awful carriage accident. During a sudden rain storm. One minute it was sunny, and the next, lightning struck and frightened the horses—some claim the coach was hit by a bolt of it. She was found with her neck broken while His Grace..." He paused and furrowed his brows. "He was thrown clear of the coach, barely a scratch on him."

Angelika inhaled softly, her gaze darting to Andrew. "How awful. No wonder he fears being out of doors."

"That was twenty-five years ago, my lady," Pruitt said in a quiet voice. "I was valet to his father, the seventh duke, at the time. His Grace went to his grave saying his son would never recover. That he felt too much guilt, or that he must have experienced something awful when he was tossed from the coach."

Angelika wondered at the mention of guilt. Surely the duke didn't think it was his fault his mother had died. "I cannot imagine experiencing such a horrendous accident and not being haunted by it for the rest of my life," she argued. "But perhaps..." She stopped and regarded Andrew with a wan grin. "Perhaps today he had decided to take a risk. To discover if being outside would be as awful as he remembered." Her brows furrowed, and a look of sadness settled on her features. "Apparently it was." Turning her attention back to the valet, she saw how worry seemed to age him, the lines in his face deepening. How his shoulders had slumped as he recounted the duke's history.

"Why do you suppose so many believe him to be... disfigured?" she asked in a quiet voice. "He is a rather handsome man." After a pause, she added, "Or is he a beast of a different sort?"

Pruitt allowed a chuckle. "I can assure you, my lady, His Grace is neither disfigured nor a beast," he replied. "However, I fear the stories of his appearance have only worsened in town because so few have actually seen him," he explained.

Bronson reappeared with the tea tray, setting a mug of broth on the nightstand near Angelika before placing the tray on the table in front of Pruitt. He poured tea for both of them.

"Should I send word to Dunfey Park about His Grace?" the butler asked as he delivered a cup to Angelika before offering the second to the valet.

"No need," Pruitt replied. "Cook saw me as I made

my way out. She'll inform the rest of the staff." He paused. "I do think it best we return him to Dunfey Park in a coach, though. I doubt he'll make it back of his own accord."

Overhearing the servants' conversation, Angelika straightened and realized the two knew one another. After so many years serving adjoining estates, she supposed they would have met in nearby Kirkby Kendal, probably at the church. "I rather doubt a coach will work," she commented, remembering Pruitt's description of the duke having been thrown from a coach as a child. "Perhaps… perhaps he merely requires a roof over his head."

"My lady?" Bronson's quizzical expression belied his usual look of boredom.

"An umbrella," she stated. "Our largest. A means to block out the sky while he walks back to Dunfey Park."

Pruitt and Bronson exchanged quick glances. "It's worth a try, for the alternative would be to transport him while he's asleep, and I rather doubt we can keep him unconscious for the entire trip," the valet replied.

"Not to mention how difficult it will be for a coach to make it through the snow," Bronson remarked. There was a road connecting the two properties, but both boasted long, tree-lined drives of nearly a quarter-mile to reach it.

"Might you have a vinaigrette?" Pruitt asked of Angelika.

She wrinkled her nose. "I shouldn't wish to subject him to such an awful odor," she replied, knowing the ammonia and parfum scents would linger in the bedchamber for a time. "Let's allow him to sleep. Surely he'll awaken of his own accord, and when he does, I'll be here. I've a book in the parlor I can read. Besides, isn't it time for the servants' luncheon?" She rather liked the idea of reading while her patient recovered but preferred to do it without the servants present.

Pruitt and Bronson exchanged curious glances. "Yes, my lady," the butler responded. He gave the valet a shrug. "Do ring if you're in need of anything."

She nodded and turned her attention back to the sleeping duke. When the servants were gone, she retrieved the French book from the parlor. Returning to the guest bedchamber, she leaned over Andrew and touched her lips to his forehead.

For that brief moment, she inhaled the scent of him and felt his warm breath wash over the bare skin above her breasts. She couldn't help but slide a thumb across his smooth forehead as her fingers speared his sandy blond hair. The silky strands remained out of place as she pulled her hand away, leaving him with a rakish appearance.

Relieved to discover he hadn't developed a fever, she settled into the chair. She had barely opened the tome when she realized she was being watched.

Glancing up, she gave a start. Andrew was staring at her, and he had the oddest expression on his face.

CHAPTER 5
A DUKE AWAKENS IN MORE
WAYS THAN ONE

A moment earlier

Andrew knew something was different the moment he realized he was in a bed and was wearing clothes. He never wore so much as a nightshirt unless it was the middle of winter and the fireplace couldn't warm his bedchamber.

The sound of voices was also unusual. On most mornings, Pruitt's voice would be urging him awake. If it wasn't his insistent words, then the incessant chirping of birds beyond his window was usually enough to wake the dead, at least in the spring.

Keeping his eyes closed, he concentrated on the conversation and had to resist the urge to wince at realizing *he* was the topic.

Pruitt was lamenting his past, another man was making suggestions, and a woman hovered nearby. The scent of her light parfum, floral and citrusy, reminded him of his mother. Especially when she leaned close and kissed him on the forehead.

Mother.

He knew she wasn't, though. This one had the voice of an angel and a touch just as soft, smoothing through his hair and along the side of his head.

There was something familiar about her.

Angel.

Making angels. In the snow.

Sure the men had departed the room, he opened his eyes and blinked a few times in an effort to focus his gaze on the woman who sat not three feet away.

The thought of seeing her every day had the oddest sensations coursing through his body. To wake up and have her be the first thing he saw would certainly be an excellent way to start the day.

Her attention wasn't on him, though, but rather on the pages of a book. A French book, with a title he struggled to interpret. Once he had, a grin formed on his lips. Either she didn't realize what she was reading, or she did, and she wasn't quite the innocent English miss he had imagined.

All at once, he knew they had been together. Outside. In the snow.

Lord Stonely's daughter.

Angelika.

He didn't intend to make a sound. Didn't intend to interrupt her reading. But his breath hitched, and she glanced up from the book.

"Your Grace!" she said in an excited whisper. She closed the book and placed it on the nightstand. "Are you feeling better?"

Andrew blinked a few times and attempted to sit up, but she placed a hand on his shoulder. "You've had a shock. It's best you don't make any sudden moves," she warned.

He relaxed back into the pillow, his gaze darting about before he once again focused on her. "Where am I?"

"In one of the guest bedchambers. In Stonefield Manor."

He ran a hand over his face and grimaced. "I suppose I went down like a sack of rocks," he murmured.

Angelika shook her head. "Actually, you fell back and made a perfect snow angel," she countered. "Most people can't fall straight back like that. They bend in the middle halfway down, or they twist about because they don't trust the snow to be soft enough."

"I am quite sure I wasn't conscious when I hit the ground," he murmured, not trying to hide his embarrassment. He really wished he could have managed to make it to wherever she was taking him without panicking. Just once in his adult life, he would have liked to have overcome his fear and do something different.

Angelika angled her head to one side. "Do you think you could sip some broth? I had Bronson bring a cup. It should still be warm." Before he could respond, she turned and retrieved the mug from the nightstand.

Andrew watched her for a moment before his attention turned to the book she had been reading. Furrowing a brow, he lifted his head and squinted, pretending to read the title on the spine. He raised a brow. "Practicing your French? Or... something else?" he asked. The barest hint of a grin accompanied his query.

Her eyes rounding in shock, Angelika swallowed. "Oh. Uh." She offered the mug to him as he pulled himself into a sitting position. "I thought to improve my French reading skills. The topic is of course unfamiliar to me."

He grinned as he took a sip of the broth. "Has it helped? With your French?" He adored seeing how her cheeks reddened with her embarrassment.

She shook her head. "I've barely begun, so I hardly know what you mean," she lied.

Nodding, he took another drink from the mug. "This was a good idea. I am rather hungry."

"Would you like to join me for luncheon? I always have cook make me a cold collation and sometimes soup on days such as this," she offered.

"I don't wish to impose any more than—"

"Oh, but you're not, Your Grace," she interrupted.

He winced. "You know who I am?" The air left him all at once.

"Mr. Pruitt told me. He saw what happened, and he and my footmen helped to bring you here."

Andrew dipped his head. "I suppose he told you of my aversion to the outdoors?"

"He did."

"You must think me ridiculous."

"Hardly, Your Grace. After what you endured?" she replied. "I lost my mother, too. When she gave birth to my younger brother. I miss her terribly."

Draining the mug, Andrew regarded her with a furrowed brow. "I hardly remember my mother," he murmured, placing the empty mug on the nightstand. He swung his legs over the opposite edge of the bed to stand, his gaze darting about in search of his shoes. He straightened his shirt sleeves. "Your father is the Marquess of Stonely, is he not?"

"He is," she affirmed, coming to her feet. "Have you met him?

"Of course. Is he about?"

"No, Your Grace. He's in London. My brother has recently returned from Greece, and they are to make their way here for Christmas. That is, once the weather allows for travel."

"You're here alone?" His expression conveyed worry as he donned his top coat and buttoned it.

She shook her head. "My younger brother is in the nursery, and there are a dozen servants about."

He seemed to relax a bit. "Have you lived here long?"

"Half my life, probably," she replied. "Ever since my brother was born, I have lived only here at Stonefield Manor."

Narrowing his eyes, Andrew regarded her with a sudden realization. "You are the hostess of the district balls, are you not?"

Rather surprised he would mention the annual fête, she said, "I am."

"I understand from my man of business that they are well planned and executed. Your father has been hosting an event that probably should have been my responsibility," he explained. "So I thank you for seeing to the details."

Angelika inhaled softly before she said, "You're welcome."

Andrew was sure she was surreptitiously studying him, perhaps his physique, when his attention was on his clothing. Even though he didn't venture out—he hadn't ridden a horse since he was six—he kept himself in good shape with exercises he could perform indoors.

On the days he and Pruitt didn't engage in a fencing match, he pounded out his frustrations on a pugilist's punching bag, ran laps around the perimeter of the ballroom, climbed a rope secured from the rafters in the attic, and ran up and down the stairs.

"I was thirteen at the time," she said, referring to her age when her mother had died.

His brows furrowed. "I seem to remember a young girl floating a boat in the pond at Dunfey Park."

Angelika's gaze dropped to her slippers. "That was me. I apologize for trespassing. I—"

"Have nothing to apologize for," he stated as he pulled on his boots. They had been placed near the fire to dry, and their warmth was welcome. "I rarely look out the windows, so it was a pleasant surprise to see someone enjoying the water. In fact, you're welcome to enjoy any part of the property. If I'm to believe my man of business, the parterre gardens are especially beautiful in the spring. My mother called it the sunset garden."

"Oh, that's the perfect name for it," she replied. "Such lovely colors. The tulips and wallflowers are all yellows and golds and oranges and reds..."

"Like a sunset," he murmured.

"Especially the ones we've been having of late," she commented. Her eyes widened. "So you *do* look out the windows," she accused, a smile brightening her face.

He chuckled. "Sometimes. As for the formal gardens, I do see them from above when I dare to look out," he commented. "I cannot imagine they are as impressive from the ground, though."

"The patterns aren't immediately apparent," she agreed. "But when you stand in the middle, it's quite beautiful."

"Perhaps I'll... venture out. This spring," he said, crossing his arms as he leaned against fireplace mantel.

"Under an umbrella, should you not wish to see the sky," she suggested.

He gave a start. He had never thought to block out what was above him with something as simple as an umbrella. "Perhaps. Or perhaps you would join me." The odd sensation he had experienced earlier, a pleasurable spasm that seemed to affect his chest, had him holding his breath.

Angelika inhaling softly. "I would like that. We'd have to do so before the Season begins, though."

"Oh?" He couldn't help the note of disappointment in his voice.

"My father has arranged for my aunt to sponsor me for my come-out. It's a bit late, I know, but I'm to stay with him in the capital while Parliament is in session," she explained. "He has a townhouse there, but no one to act as his hostess. As I do here."

"So you are not yet betrothed?" he asked. Not having met many women in his life, he had no idea of her age, but he knew better than to ask.

She shook her head. "I haven't exactly met many men."

"We have that in common," he murmured.

She stood and waved to the door. "We should probably move to the parlor, Your Grace."

He furrowed his brows. "But, why?" He glanced around, rather liking the decor of the bedchamber. There were chairs in which to sit, the fire was putting out more than enough heat, and there were no servants about. "It appears tea has already been brought," he commented, his gaze captured by the biscuits.

Angelika inhaled to respond and then stood. "Would you like a cup?"

"Indeed," he replied, hoping his growling stomach wasn't audible.

"How do you take it?"

"No sugar or milk," he replied.

She made her way to the low table where the tea tray was set and poured him a cup. "It's not really proper for me to be... alone... with a man. Without a chaperone," she stammered as she handed him the cup and saucer. "Biscuit?" she offered.

He plucked a lemon biscuit from the plate and placed it on his saucer, his brows furrowing when he saw her hand was trembling. "You needn't fear me, Angel," he said. "I am not a... not the beast I have come to learn some think I am."

"Oh, it's not that, Your Grace," she replied. "It's not that at all."

He blinked, one brow furrowing even deeper. "I introduced myself as Andrew hoping you would call me that," he said.

Angelika blinked. "Your Grace? But now that I know you are the duke—"

"Andrew," he stated.

She seemed about to put voice to a protest and thought better of it. "Then I shall call you Andrew."

"I will not take advantage," he said, heartened when she displayed a momentary look of disappointment. "Except maybe to ask for another biscuit." He gave her a grin that had his eyes twinkling with mischief.

Her eyes darted to the side before she allowed a titter. "You may have all of them if you'd like," she said as she held out the plate. "Please, do make yourself comfortable." Apparently realizing he would not do so until she settled into a chair, she retrieved her tea from the nightstand and joined him by the fire.

He had already eaten his first biscuit when he took a steadying breath and let it out. "Would you be so kind as to tell me what it is you have heard about me?"

Her mouth formed an 'o' before a scoff sounded. "I would hardly be kind to repeat—"

"Please."

Blinking, she set her cup and saucer on the table and sighed. "I have heard you were terribly disfigured. So ugly you could not go out in public, which is why you are never seen outside of Dunfey Park," she said. "Which is ridiculous, because..." She stopped, her cheeks once again reddening with embarrassment.

"Because?" he prompted.

"Well, because... well... you're rather handsome," she stammered.

Recoiling as if he'd been slapped across the face, Andrew grinned. "Oh! And what's this about a beast?"

Angelika's mouth opened and closed several times before she lifted a shoulder. "There's been talk in town that you're a beast. I'm not sure if it's because they thought you might *look* like a beast or if it's because they thought you *behaved* like one, but... that's what they say."

He made an odd sound in the back of his throat and leaned back in his chair. Did she think him capable of such poor behavior? Now that she had met him? Now that she had spent time in his company? "I am not a beast. I would never behave as one, unless someone did something unforgivable," he murmured. "To someone I cared about."

"I know," she replied.

"So... if you do not fear me, then why must we have a chaperone?" He paused when he realized she was about to rise from the chair, her hands gripping the arms so her knuckles were white.

"I fear what *I* will do, Andrew. Again," she whispered.

The duke blinked before his gaze darted about the room. "Did you...?"

"Kiss you. Yes," she admitted. "In the guise of

determining if you had a fever, but..." She swallowed. "Yes."

He recoiled slightly. "You kissed my forehead. I dreamt that was my mother," he whispered. "Your scent is the same as hers."

Angelika seemed to have trouble breathing as she dipped her head. "Is that how she discovered if you had a fever?"

He nodded. "Will you do it again? I'm feeling rather feverish."

CHAPTER 6
A KISS LEADS TO SO
MUCH MORE

*A*ngelika let out the breath she had been holding and rose from her chair. Andrew met her halfway as she stood on tiptoes and he bent his head. He closed his eyes as her lips collided with the center of his forehead. A moment later, and they were trailing over his eyelids, along his cheekbones and finally to his mouth.

When their lips touched, there was a moment's hesitation.

"I have never done this before," he murmured, his lips brushing over hers.

"Neither have I," she countered.

He couldn't stop his grin of amusement as his arms wrapped around her shoulders and waist while one of her hands went to his cheek.

Their kisses were tentative at first, the lush pillows of her lips cushioning the harder surface of his. Soon, her soft purrs joined his throaty moans as their mouths opened and the kisses deepened. When their tongues touched, they both gave a start and the kiss suddenly ended.

Angelika blinked several times as she fought to regain her bearings while Andrew lowered his forehead to hers and struggled to catch his breath.

"I would not object to doing that again," she whispered.

Andrew chuckled softly, not bothering to reply as he recaptured her lips with his. This time, there was no need to be tentative. No need to be timid. He slipped his tongue between her lips, explored her teeth until her tongue tangled with his. When her purrs increased to moans, he moved his lips over her cheeks, along her jawline, and down her neck to where her pulse pounded.

Elsewhere, his manhood lengthened and thickened behind the placket of his breeches. The desire to undo the fastenings and allow it to escape had him ending the kiss with a soft curse.

"What is it?" she asked, her eyes glazed over.

"I... I... if I don't stop, I shall ruin you quite thoroughly," he warned in a whisper. "And then you will be stuck with me for the rest of your days."

Angelika slid a hand along the side of his face and then to the back of his neck, her fingernails scraping the nape as she pressed her body against his. A shiver shot through his spine, and he inhaled sharply.

"You say that as if I shouldn't want to be stuck with you," she countered.

He once again dropped his forehead to hers. "I am a recluse. I do not go out. My home is a prison, and I shouldn't want it to be the same for you."

She lifted her gaze to meet his. "Would you allow me to spend time in the gardens? To go to the folly and the pond? To go to town for shopping? To come here to pay a call on my family?"

Swallowing, he considered her queries. "Of course. But I do not believe I could go with you."

"I understand."

"Mayhap we could share time in the sunset gardens," he offered. "With an umbrella over my head," he added.

She gave him a brilliant smile. "I look forward to it."

He furrowed a brow. "There is such joy in you. When you make angels, you are positively incandescent."

Angelika continued to smile as heat suffused her face. "Imagine what I might be like when I make love to you," she teased.

The comment almost sounded like a dare, and Andrew's eyes darkened. "Something else I have not done," he whispered.

She swallowed. "Neither have I."

He glanced over at the book on the nightstand. "But you've read about it?"

Heat once again colored her cheeks. "I looked at the color plates, mostly," she admitted. "I understand what goes where. What happens," she added in a breathy voice.

"I should like to learn with you," he whispered.

"Right now?" she asked in awe.

He swallowed. "Do you need a few minutes?"

She tittered. "No, but..." Her eyes rounded. "The servants have no doubt finished their luncheon by now," she whispered. "Mr. Pruitt will come to see if you're awake."

"We'll leave a note on the door," he said.

Blinking, Angelika asked, "Saying what?"

"Do not disturb. Betrothed couple... coupling?" he offered with a guffaw.

"Andrew!" she scolded.

He sobered "You will be mine? My wife? My duchess?" he whispered.

Angelika wondered at the sound of uncertainty in his words. "I will be yours. And you will be mine." She said this last in a voice filled with warning.

His arms were like steel bands as they wrapped around her back and pulled her hard against him. His lips once again claimed hers in a crushing kiss that left them both breathless as they began to undo buttons and knots and bows and laces. Drapes were drawn, and with the fireplace providing the only light, the room took on a darkness tinged with gold.

With him wearing only a shirt and her a chemise, the two tumbled onto the bed. The frantic movements of only a moment ago were replaced with tentative touches and deep kisses, soft breaths and softer murmurs.

When Andrew saw the silhouette of her ruched nipples through the fabric of her chemise, he brushed a thumb over one as he suckled the other, delighting in hearing her inhalations of breath.

When she slid a hand down the front of his body, her fingers traced the contours of his muscles through the blond hair that covered his chest down to where his manhood jutted from a nest of darker curls. She stared in awe as it seemed to move of its own accord with her every touch.

Before she had finished drawing a finger down its throbbing vein, she gave a sound of protest when Andrew pushed her back to the bed. The sound changed to one of appreciation when he skimmed a hand down her belly, his fingers spearing her mons until they pressed into her wet folds.

She jerked beneath his hold, gasping when the fingers touched her engorged womanhood. Her quiet "yes" and the way she tilted her hips and opened her thighs emboldened him to do more. Rubbing her harder, he thrilled at hearing her quiet pleas for more until her body quaked and quivered and one of her hands moved to still his.

He was atop her in only a moment, one hand cupping a globe of her bottom while he used the other to hold himself over her. The tip of his manhood poked into her entrance even before the sharp darts of pleasure had run their course, and in three tentative thrusts, he was buried in her.

Angelika inhaled, her chest lifting from the bed as his lips captured hers for a brief kiss.

"Does it hurt?" he asked in a whisper.

She shook her head. "I don't think so. Does it hurt you?" Lifting her knees to press them into the sides of his thighs, she sighed. "Oh, that's much better," she whispered.

He had to suppress the urge to chuckle. "I have never felt anything so wonderful in my entire life."

"I'm not sure what to do." Her hands slid to the sides of his chest as if seeking a good place to hold on.

Andrew dropped his head almost to her shoulder. "You're tickling me," he said, his lips taking purchase on hers for a quick kiss.

"Oh, I didn't mean to. I don't know where to put my hands." When he pulled out of her, nearly all of the way, she made a sound of protest and gripped his hips. "Don't go."

He thrust into her, causing the ropes beneath the mattress to groan nearly as much as he did.

Understanding what to do, Angelika met his next thrust with an upward thrust of her hips. She delighted in hearing his soft curse of surprise as his sac collided with her quim. When he continued his thrusts, each one a bit quicker than the one before, she matched his rhythm and clenched hard on his manhood.

Unable to stave off his release, Andrew thrust into her one more time and stilled his movements. The spasm that gripped his body had his entire torso rising, the cords of his neck showing in relief as his head lifted.

Angelika watched in awe and inhaled sharply when she felt his release at her core. The wash of warmth flooded her insides as Andrew's body remained suspended over hers. Then all at once, he seemed free of whatever had held him, and he relaxed atop her.

Wrapping her arms around his back, she held onto him until his breathing returned to normal. "Are you... are you all right?" she asked in a panicked whisper.

"Oh, yes. We're doing this again," he replied, finally lifting his head to regard her with a grin.

She gave him a brilliant smile. "I should think so," she replied. "It's a perfect activity for a cold afternoon. I'm all warm and—"

"You're shivering," he countered, his expression changing to concern.

"Not from cold, I assure you," she countered. "I'm simply excited is all. When do you suppose we can do it again?"

He chuckled as he rolled off of her. "I need a few minutes to recover, I think," he said. "Mayhap more." He glanced over at her, his grin matching hers until he suddenly sobered. "You... you may have bled a bit," he warned.

"Oh, I expect so," she replied.

"We should wait until you're recovered."

She inhaled deeply. "I'll certainly recover faster with some food. I'm definitely hungry. Are you?"

"Starving," he claimed. He clasped one of her hands in his own and brought it to his lips. "I think we shall be very happy together," he murmured.

She rolled onto her side and kissed him. "I agree."

CHAPTER 7
A BETROTHAL OR TWO

en minutes later

"I feel as if I can barely stand," Angelika remarked as Andrew struggled to do up the laces of her stays. "Like my bones have turned to jelly."

"I think I know what you mean," he replied, helping her into her petticoats. He had already pulled on his breeches and waistcoat, although the buttons remained undone. "I shall sleep very well this evening."

She grinned as she did up his buttons, barely finishing the last before he had her gown falling down over her shoulders. "What happens now, do you suppose?"

Andrew furrowed a brow. "I should speak with your father. Set a date. The banns will need to be read, and then..." He stopped and swallowed. "Oh, dear."

"What is it?" she asked in alarm.

"We'll have to be married in the church," he whispered.

Angelika swallowed, immediately understanding his concern. "Is there a chapel in Dunfey Park?"

He nodded.

"Well, you're a duke. Surely the parson can marry us there," she reasoned. She helped him into his top coat and then buttoned it.

"Perhaps," he hedged. He saw to the buttons on the back of her gown, his fingers tangling with the curls at the nape of her neck. When he finished, he pushed aside her hair and kissed the tender skin.

She giggled. "You're tickling me," she accused.

He turned her around and inhaled softly. "You're positively glowing," he remarked.

Reaching a hand up to his cheek, she stood on tiptocs and kissed him. "All thanks to you, my betrothed."

He reached for his boots and was about to pull one on when there was a knock at the door.

Angelika gasped and quickly straightened the bed linens before she called out, "Come."

Pruitt opened the door and peeked in, his gaze immediately going to his master. "Your Grace. I am so relieved you're awake."

"I'm glad to be awake," Andrew said, holding out his boot. "You have timed your arrival perfectly."

Hurrying to kneel before the duke, Pruitt saw to pushing the footwear onto the duke's feet as Angelika surreptitiously shoved her own feet into her slippers.

"How was the luncheon, Mr. Pruitt?" she asked, returning the chair she had been sitting in earlier to its usual spot.

"Oh, very good, my lady," the valet responded. "Bronson was wondering if you would be going down for your own luncheon?"

"I am, as is His Grace. He's has awakened hungry, and I shall not allow him to return to Dunfey Park on an empty stomach."

"Very good, my lady," he replied.

"I have news to share," Andrew announced.

Pruitt stood and regarded the duke a moment, his brows furrowing when he saw the state of his master's cravat.

"Oh," Andrew said, lowering his chin. "I took it off. I crushed it whilst I was sleeping, and I'm rot at retying it."

Angelika tittered. "*That* is your news?"

He chuckled. "We're betrothed for only a few minutes, and you're already teasing me?" he countered, reaching out to pull her to his side. "Pruitt, I'm getting married to Lady Angelika."

About to wrap the repleated silk cravat around Andrew's neck, Pruitt froze and stared at him. "Betrothed, Your Grace?"

The duke nodded happily. "We'll marry as soon as the banns are read, and after I speak with Lord Stonely, of course."

His head shaking from side to side, Pruitt's gaze darted from the duke to Angelika and back to the duke. "But, you cannot, Your Grace. You're already betrothed."

CHAPTER 8
A BROTHER TELLS WHAT HE KNOWS

The silence that followed the valet's pronouncement was so loud, Angelika wondered if she had fainted. She was sure her heart had stopped beating. Her breathing certainly had. Now stars were dancing about in front of her eyes as gray threatened to take her vision.

Andrew's voice kept her in the here and now, or rather the tone of it. She'd had yet to hear him angry, and at that moment, he was livid.

"How *dare* you mention Lady Phoebe," Andrew said in a quiet voice filled with menace.

"Who?" Angelika managed to get out, glad for the duke's body. If it hadn't been for him, she would have ended up crumpled on the floor.

"Lady Phoebe," Pruitt whispered, wincing when

Andrew jerked. One of his fists was clenched into a ball.

Unable to put a face to the name, Angelika swallowed. The rushing sound in her ears prevented her from hearing anything else, and she did the only thing she could—ran from the room.

She nearly collided with Bronson, whose eyes rounded in alarm.

"Your luncheon is ready, my lady," he said.

"I do not believe I could keep it down," she said, heading for the stairs. She wasn't sure where she was going, but at that moment, she had to be as far away from the Duke of Suffolk as possible. When her vision blurred, she realized she was crying.

How could he?

How could he claim he would marry her and take her virtue when he was already betrothed to someone else?

She had climbed two flights of stairs before she realized it, her labored breathing made more so with her tears.

Richard.

Although he was too young to understand, he would sit quietly and listen. He might ask a few questions, but they would be easy to answer.

She burst into the nursery, tears streaming down her

face, to discover her brother at his desk, writing on a slate with a piece of chalk.

Mrs. Cooper turned from her own slate. "Lady Angelika? What is wrong?"

Angelika stared at the nurse for a moment before she said, "I am in need of my brother. Will you excuse him from his lessons?"

The nurse, already coming to her feet to perform a curtsy, said, "Of course, my lady." Turning to the boy, she said, "Go with your sister. We'll resume this lesson when you return."

Richard beamed in delight before he sobered and stood. "Where are we going?" he asked.

Angelika's shoulders slumped. "The library. We need *Debrett's*." Surely they could determine the identity of Lady Phoebe from the book featuring the names of everyone in the peerage. How many Phoebes of marriageable age could there be?

Blinking, her brother stood and joined her at the door. "I cannot yet read most names," he warned.

"No, but you can listen," she countered as they made their way down the stairs.

"Is it true the Duke of Suffolk is in residence?" he asked.

Angelika nearly stumbled on the first step. "How do you know that?"

He gave her a quelling glance. "I'm not deaf," he said with a huff. "I overheard Cook mention it to Mrs. Cooper when she delivered my luncheon," he added. "She was quite excited."

The mention of luncheon had her stomach growling. Spotting Thompkins at the end of the second story hall, she called out, "Have my luncheon brought to the library, will you please?"

The footman blinked and bowed. "Yes, my lady." He hurried off toward the servants' stairs as she and Richard made their way down to the first floor.

"What's happened to make you cry?" he asked, allowing her to grip one of his hands in his. The other slid along the top of the bannister, leaving chalk dust trails as they descended.

Pausing on the threshold to regard her brother with a look of surprise, Angelika sniffled. "The duke proposed marriage, and I accepted, and then his valet said he couldn't marry me because he's already betrothed to Lady Phoebe," she blurted.

Richard seemed to think on her answer for a time before he said, "So he's not some sort of beast?"

She blinked and scoffed. "Not like *you're* imagining," she said as she urged him into the library. Only a few doors away was the guest bedchamber where she had left Andrew and his valet. "And he's not the least bit disfigured." Even as she made the comment, she was remembering his naked body. After they had made love, he had pulled off his shirt and then held her in his arms.

He was not disfigured in the least. His body was like that of one of the Greek statues her mother had ordered for the back garden. As for his face, well, he was more handsome than he had any right to be.

Oh, Andrew.

Apparently her body hadn't sorted the news of his betrayal, for frissons of pleasure suddenly darted about beneath her skin.

Less than hour ago, she had been incandescently happy. Experiencing pleasures she could never imagine. Imparting pleasure without even understanding how. Speaking of a future with Andrew had made her realize life with a recluse might be lonely, but the freedom he would grant her would more than make up for his need to remain indoors.

Richard's hand waving in front of her face had her giving a start. "What?"

He rolled his eyes. "You're obviously in love with him," he said. "So why are we going to look him up in *Debrett's*?"

About to deny his supposition, Angelika let her last

breath out in a *whoosh*. "His valet says he's betrothed to Lady Phoebe," she whispered.

His dark brows furrowing, Richard crossed his arms in a way that made him look like a younger version of his father. Despite her mood, Angelika nearly tittered.

"Lady Phoebe isn't going to marry the duke," Richard stated.

About to pull the latest edition of *Debrett's Peerage and Baronetage* from a shelf, Angelika paused and stared at her brother. "What?"

"Lady Phoebe isn't going to marry the duke," her brother repeated.

"How do you know this?"

"Because she promised Robert she would marry *him* when he returned from his Grand Tour," he replied.

Angelika blinked as she stared at him. "How... how is it you know this?" she asked, never having learned her older brother had a woman in mind to be his eventual marchioness. As far as she knew, he hadn't been courting anyone after he completed university. "And are we speaking of the same Lady Phoebe?"

Richard shrugged. "Robert danced with her at the district ball before he left for Greece," he said. "She was complaining that she was betrothed since birth to a beast, and she claimed she had no intention of marrying him."

"The district ball?" Angelika repeated. "The one we hosted before Robert left for Greece?"

Richard settled onto the leather couch and stared at her in disbelief. "You hosted it," he claimed. "Or father did. You always say I'm too young to attend, but I told you at dinner I was watching from the top of the stairs," he added with a wicked grin. "And some other places during the evening."

Angelika wasn't about to tell him he was still too young to attend district balls, but thought better of it. He had information she needed. "Go on," she said.

"I might have only been five at the time, but I remember it quite well. I saw Mr. Cooper from the draper store kiss my nurse."

Angelika stared at her brother for a long time before she said, "That's because your nurse and Mr. Cooper are married."

Richard blinked before his eyes rounded. "Ewww," he said in disgust.

"Tell me more about Robert and Lady Phoebe," she ordered, gasping when Bronson appeared with her luncheon on a tray.

Behind him was Andrew, his expression unreadable.

Richard glanced up at the duke and immediately came to his feet, apparently aware the man was someone of importance.

Dipping a deep curtsy, Angelika kept her eyes downcast as Bronson placed the tray on the library table and then bowed before taking his leave. "Your Grace," she murmured.

"Yes, do tell us more about your older brother and Lady Phoebe," Andrew said, his words directed to the boy. "You are Lord Richard, I presume?"

Richard bowed. "Your Grace," he said, struggling not to topple onto his head. "It's very good to make your acquaintance."

Despite his serious manner, Andrew smirked. "You were saying?"

His gaze darting to his sister, Richard waited until she waved a hand. "His Grace told you to continue," she whispered hoarsely.

Richard took an exaggerated deep breath. "My brother Robert kissed Lady Phoebe during the district ball and asked if she would be his wife," he blurted. "Told her they would marry when he returned from his Grand Tour, and then he kissed her again," he added, his face screwed up in a grimace.

Angelika straightened, her gaze immediately going to Andrew. "Is he speaking of the same Lady Phoebe?" she asked in a quiet voice.

"If she is the daughter of the current Earl of Appleby, then yes," he replied.

"So... you *have* met her?" If Andrew never left his house, then Lady Phoebe would have had to pay a call on him at Dunfey Park to make his acquaintance.

"I have *not*. The earl's estate is about ten miles from here. He and my father were good friends back in their day."

"Did you know about the betrothal?"

Andrew winced. "I remember when my father informed me—I think I was twelve at the time." He paused when Angelika suddenly sobbed. He took a step in her direction, intending to take her hand. When she took a matching step back, a look of pain crossed his face. "He had made arrangements with Appleby as a means of shoring up the ducal accounts with a generous dowry. But..." He dipped his head. "I received a letter from her two years ago asking if I would be so kind as to release her from the agreement. She had met someone who wished to marry her—"

"My brother, Robert," Richard interrupted.

The duke acknowledged the boy's comment with an arched brow. "Apparently so. She did not mention a name, and I thought she merely wished to break off our betrothal because she had come to believe the rumors about me," Andrew explained. "Thought me to be a beast or... horribly disfigured."

Angelika swallowed another sob. "Of which you are

neither," she whispered. In a louder voice, she asked, "Does the dukedom still require her dowry?"

Giving a start, Andrew said, "No. No. Our accounts are in good stead."

"Did you...?" She couldn't finish the question, fearing how he would answer.

"I wrote back releasing her from our betrothal, and I promised to send best wishes when I learned of her new betrothal. I heard nothing after that."

Angelika left out the breath she'd been holding. "Oh."

"I have set Pruitt straight on the matter, and he is sorry for having caused consternation."

"Oh, Andrew," she whispered.

"Andrew?" Richard repeated, his shocked gaze darting between his sister and the duke. "Who's Andrew?"

The duke allowed a teasing grin. "If you find kissing abhorrent, you'd best close your eyes, future brother," he warned.

Richard blinked. "What does abhorrent mean?"

Andrew had already gathered Angelika into his arms and was kissing her quite thoroughly, which had Richard emitting a sound of disgust as he fled the library.

When Andrew finally came up for air, he gazed

down on Angelika with an expression of humor. "Probably not the best impression to leave with the poor boy," he murmured.

"Oh, he'll get past it," she countered. "And probably seek you out for advice when he experiences his first crush."

Andrew burst out laughing. "You say that as if you think I have any experience in the matter?"

She gave him a prim grin. "Do you consider *me* a crush?"

He sobered and once again drew her in for a kiss. "Well, I certainly fell for you, even if it was into the snow," he replied. "I may fall again if I don't get something to eat."

Angelika stood on tiptoes and kissed him. "Then join me for a luncheon? We can eat right here," she offered as she pulled him to the library table where Bronson had left a tray of food featuring sliced meats, cheese and bread.

"You are the consummate hostess," he remarked, holding a chair for her.

She beamed in delight as she sat and they shared a late afternoon meal.

CHAPTER 9
ANGEL DUST WORKS ITS
MAGIC

An hour later

Darkness descended over wintery Westmorland, leaving the fireplace in the library the only source of light. The remains of their late luncheon had been removed by Bronson, replaced with a tray featuring a glass of port and a glass of claret. Once the spirits had been drunk, the two newly betrothed had settled onto the couch.

"I should head back to Dunfey Park," Andrew said in a quiet voice.

"Under the protection of an umbrella," Angelika said. "Would you like me to walk with you?" she offered. "I wouldn't mind."

Andrew regarded her with an expression of surprise. "It will be very dark by the time we arrive and then..."

He stopped speaking as an eyebrow lifted. "Oh, I think I understand what *you're* proposing," he accused as a grin lifted his lips.

Smirking, Angelika shrugged. "I understand if you'd prefer I return here after I've seen to your safe arrival at Dunfey Park. We can have a footman follow us," she suggested. "Just to be sure we make it there."

"On a cold night like this?" he countered. "I will not have you traipsing through the snow both ways. No. You'll stay the night at Dunfey Park. About time I scandalize my servants."

Angelika tittered. "I can pack a valise with some clothes, and once we're there, you can show me to the mistress suite."

He frowned. "It will be terribly cold in there," he warned.

"Well, I've no intention of sleeping in there," she countered. Lifting her head from his shoulder, she noticed his amusement fade. "What is it?"

"Your father is going to be—"

"Relieved, and more than happy to hand over my dowry to you."

He furrowed his blond brows. "Why do you say that?"

She allowed an exaggerated sigh. "Father arranged for his sister to sponsor me for my come-out in London this spring, which means a modiste was going to have to make one of those preposterous and expensive court gowns and an entire wardrobe for the Season," she explained. "You will have saved him and my aunt from the expense and the trouble."

"You've been his hostess ever since your mother died," he stated. "Unless he's taken a wife during his latest trip to London, he's not going to be happy about losing your skills in arranging the annual district ball or all of his dinner parties."

Angelika inhaled to ask how he knew about the dinner parties when she remembered he was always on the guest list. Invited but sure to send his regrets.

"Is there a ballroom at Dunfey Park?"

"There is," he acknowledged. "And a huge dining room with a table that can seat twenty-four comfortably."

She grinned. "It sounds as if *you're* going to be taking on the hosting duties for the district ball."

He allowed a grimace and sighed. "Only if you continue as hostess," he agreed.

She gave him a brilliant smile. "Father will be so relieved." At the duke's look of surprise, she added, "He despises having to play host. He only does it because I insist."

Andrew chuckled softly before he sobered. "We

should probably be going," he suggested. "With any luck, it's clear outside." From what had happened earlier that day, he was sure clouds were the reason he sought refuge indoors. Clouds brought rain, and rain brought thunder and lightning, and lightning... He cleared his throat in an effort to keep a lump from forming there.

"If it's clear, the stars will look like diamonds," Angelika said. She stood and helped him up from the couch. "We'll be able to see the Milky Way, and the snow will be perfect to make an—"

"Angel," he said in a warning voice. "I'll be staying under an umbrella," he reminded her.

"Oh, of course," she agreed, managing to hide her momentary disappointment.

"However, should *you* be overcome with the need to make a snow angel, you can, of course," he said. "I'll even help you out of the snow."

She giggled. "It should only take me a few minutes to pack a valise. Bronson will have your greatcoat dried by now."

"I'll find Pruitt," he said.

The two took their leave of the library and found one another ten minutes later in the vestibule. Pruitt and Styles were both dressed for the weather while Bronson stood by with the household's largest umbrella. He handed it to the duke after he had his coat and gloves pulled on, and Angelika gave her valise to Styles.

"I'm off for a tour of Dunfey Park, but I shan't return until tomorrow," she said. "Bronson, you're in charge," she added.

"Yes, my lady."

She and Andrew made their way out of the house, immediately finding the tracks that led to Dunfey Park. Despite the dark, the snow seemed to provide its own illumination, helped along by a half-moon rising in the east. Ahead of them, Styles carried her valise and Pruitt held up a lantern.

"It's so still," she commented, white puffs forming in front of her face. "The air looks as if it has glitter in it."

His attention on the path before them, Andrew appreciated Angelika's attempt to keep his mind off the obvious.

Especially when they passed the impression he had left in the snow earlier that day.

"Your snow angel," she said in delight.

"It doesn't have much in the way of wings," he said, wincing at seeing the trampled snow on either side of it. The sleeves of his great coat had supplied some semblance of an arch, but it ended at the shoulders.

When Angelika didn't respond, he glanced over to

discover she was looking up. He heard her inhale softly and noticed how she slowed her steps.

The wonder on her face had him dropping the umbrella back enough to see what had her so mesmerized. Arcing across the sky above them was a wide band of stars that glowed against the black backdrop, as if a jeweler had dumped all his diamonds onto a sheet of black velvet. Andrew slowly turned, his gaze following the band until it disappeared below the horizon. "The Milky Way?" he guessed in awe.

"Indeed," Angelika replied. "Oh!"

"What is it?"

She pointed up to where a falling star was leaving a brilliant white trail behind it. "A shooting star," she exclaimed, her finger pointed to the south. "You have to make a wish."

"A wish?" he repeated. His gaze was still on where the last of the star's streamer had disappeared.

"Yes, but you cannot say what it is or it won't come true," she explained, resuming the trek towards Dunfey Park.

Andrew chuckled as they passed the line of poplar trees. "I suppose that means you won't be sharing your wish with me."

She gave him a dubious glance and grinned, hiding her surprise when he didn't immediately raise the umbrella back up over his head. "There will probably be another I can make a wish on," she reasoned. "I wished for us to be happy in marriage is all."

After hearing her wish, Andrew thought his rather selfish, but he didn't put voice to it—that he wished he could go outdoors without feeling panicked. "I believe that will be a given," he murmured. "At least it will be for me."

She beamed in delight, their progress through the snow less cumbersome now that the land had evened out and the snow wasn't so deep.

He lowered the umbrella so he could once again see the sky above. "It does humble a person, does it not?" he asked so only she could hear. The servants were well ahead of them now, obviously eager to reach Dunfey Park, while clouds of white surrounded their heads with their every breath.

"What do you mean?" she asked as she followed his gaze.

"This huge night sky. It's like the interior of a giant black dome. Doesn't it make you feel small?"

She shrugged. "I suppose," she agreed.

"It does me, although it's also... so far away. Unless it drops a falling star on me, it cannot... it cannot hurt me."

Regarding him with awe for a moment, Angelika

allowed her gaze to sweep across the expanse of black and stars. "I understand what you mean," she said quietly. "Will you help me up?"

"What?" he asked.

Grinning, she fell back into the powdery snow and giggled as she flailed her arms and legs in the snow.

Letting out a guffaw, Andrew reached down and offered a hand. "Come here, my Angel." He dropped the umbrella and helped her to stand. After brushing the snow from the back of her redingote, he pulled her into his arms. Their kiss might have continued long into the night, but crystals had begun falling, landing on the tips of their eyelashes.

"Snow?" he said in surprise, blinking several times as he looked up. The sky was still clear, though, and he chuckled softly.

"Angel dust," she countered happily. "Isn't it magical?"

He gave a start. "Are you casting a spell on me?" he accused in a voice filled with suspicion.

She dipped her head, noticing the open umbrella resting in the snow. Through her crystal-tipped lashes, she said, "I thought I already had." Lifting the umbrella, she closed it, then hooked her arm into his.

They hurried through the snow, laughing as they burst into Dunfey Park.

CHAPTER 10
EPILOGUE

*Two Sundays later, Christmas Eve, in Lord
Stonely's study at Stonefield Manor*

"I cannot decide if I should admonish you for having ruined my only daughter, or if I should double her dowry, Your Grace," Mark, Marquess of Stonely, stated before handing Andrew a glass of brandy.

Beyond the study's only window, water dripped from the manor's eves as the snow on the roof melted in the bright sunshine.

"I am quite prepared to *be* admonished," the duke replied. "I now understand how it is a proper gentleman can succumb to a dose of angel dust and find himself irrevocably, deeply, and madly in love. As for her dowry, whatever you have set aside will be acceptable."

Although the banns had only been read twice during

the past two Sunday services—which had those in Kirkby Kendal all abuzz with wonder—Angelika had already taken on the running of the Dunfey Park household. She continued to see to Stonefield Manor in the middle of the day.

"Truth be told, I thought you were betrothed to someone else, or I might have introduced you and Angel years ago," Mark responded.

"Oh, I was. Lady Phoebe broke it off, which is a good thing since she's betrothed to your son."

Mark winced. "Something I learned only a few weeks ago when I collected him from the ship that brought him back from the Mediterranean," he said. "Robert barely arrived here before he took off to pay a call on her father." His eyes suddenly widened. "Wait. How is it you know about his betrothal?"

Andrew chuckled softly. "It seems your younger son paid witness to their betrothal at one of the district balls you hosted here at your house."

"Ah," the marquess replied, sitting back in his chair. "Richard is rather resourceful when it comes to gathering information."

"He's quite... knowledgable about the goings on here and over at Dunfey Park," Andrew hedged, "which suggests he may have borrowed your spy glass."

Mark's eyes once again rounded as he glanced over

to where a telescope should have been mounted near his window. "I've a mind to recommend him to Chamberlain at the Foreign Office. He could be a master spy," he groused.

Chuckling, Andrew said, "An acceptable position for a second son, I should think." He finally relaxed. His worry about the marquess' reaction to his request for Angelika's hand had been needless, especially when he reminded Stonely there would be no need for her to have a Season in London with the requisite wardrobe and presentation to the queen.

Angling his head to one side, Mark said, "I cannot tell you how surprised I was when Bronson told me of your arrival. I understood from our past meetings that you never leave Dunfey Park."

"Until a bit over a week ago, I didn't," Andrew admitted.

"What's happened to change that?"

Andrew inhaled to answer before dipping his head. "A snow angel appeared in my back garden, and before I knew it, I was falling for her. Quite literally."

Mark smirked. "You had a soft landing, I hope?"

Once again chuckling, Andrew said, "Yes, but I left quite an impression." Having passed by the location of his snow angel only a half-hour earlier, he was relieved to see the evidence of it nearly gone in the melting snow.

Meanwhile, his other snow angel was making an impression on the Dunfey Park staff. He had worried she might not be welcomed by his housekeeper and the cook when in fact they seemed relieved to have someone seeing to menus and the household accounts. They were especially happy to be creating wreaths and sprays to decorate Dunfey Park for Christmas. The entire ground floor had smelled of pine boughs when he departed the hour prior, and before he had made it past the parterre garden, he passed two footmen who were lugging a yule log into the house.

Seeing him leave through the front door had one of the footmen so shocked, he nearly dropped his end of the log.

"So, when will you wed?" Mark asked.

"New Year's Day, if you'll allow it."

"Of course I'll allow it, but..." the marquess shook his head. "Perhaps Lady Phoebe can be coerced into a quick wedding. Unless you're going to allow Angel to continue running both households, Stonefield will require a new lady of the house."

"Or perhaps *you* could take a wife," Andrew suggested, arching a brow.

Mark let out a guffaw. "I rather doubt I'm going to

find a spinster or a widow of the *ton* willing to live so far from London," he said.

"I discovered one doesn't have to go far to find one's very own angel," Andrew countered. "There is probably one ready to fall for you in Kirkby Kendal." He set aside his empty glass and stood. "And I rather doubt you'll have to make a snow angel to prove yourself."

Coming to his feet, Mark gave the duke a look of confusion before he shook hands with him. "I can't imagine what kind of impression that might make on a lady," he remarked.

Grinning, Andrew said, "The very best kind, it seems. At least it did for me." He gave a nod. "Good day."

Mark watched his future son-in-law take his leave, a vision of angels dancing in his head.

AUTHOR NOTES

What is the origin of snow angels?

According to legend, the first snow angels came from medieval Jewish mystics who would roll around in the snow to "purge themselves from evil urges."

The earliest known reference to the activity in print dates back to 1799. British poet and travel-writer Thomas Pennant mentioned snow angels in his book "Recollections of a Tour Made in Scotland."

Meanwhile, the tradition of children making snow angels had become common in Norwegian culture.

Andrew's ailment

Although it should be clear Andrew suffers from agoraphobia, an anxiety disorder where a person is afraid to leave a place of safety, the condition wasn't first diagnosed until 1871 by Karl Friedrich Otto Westphal. He coined the term after observing patients who exhibited severe anxiety when traveling to certain public areas of Berlin.

Your Invitation!

Do you crave historical romance filled with passion and red hot chemistry?

Come join me and my author friends in the Facebook group, Historical Harlots, for exclusive giveaways, chats with amazing HistRom authors, raunchy shenanigans, and more! **https://www.facebook.com/groups/2102138599813601**

ABOUT THE AUTHOR

A self-described nerd and student of history, Linda Rae spent many years as a published technical writer specializing in 3D graphics workstations, software and 3D animation (her movie credits include SHREK and SHREK 2). Getting lost in the rabbit holes of research has resulted in historical romances set in the Regency-era as well as Ancient Greece.

A fan of action-adventure movies, she can frequently be found at the local cinema. Although she no longer has any tropical fish, she follows the San Jose Sharks and makes her home in Cody, Wyoming.

For more information:
www.lindaraesande.com
Sign up for Linda Rae's newsletter:
Regency Romance with a Twist
Follow Linda Rae's blog:
Regency Romance with a Twist